S0-DQV-836

Merry Christmas, Anna Hibiscus!

Merry Christmas, ANNA HIBISCUS!

Atinuke

illustrated by Lauren Tobia

CANDLEWICK PRESS

First Candlewick Press edition 2023
First US edition published by Kane Miller 2011
First published by Walker Books (UK) 2010

Library of Congress Catalog Card Number 2022922831
ISBN 978-1-5362-3121-2 (hardcover)
ISBN 978-1-5362-3122-9 (paperback)

23 24 25 26 27 28 LBM 10 9 8 7 6 5 4 3 2 1

Printed in Melrose Park, IL, USA

This book was typeset in Stempel Schneider and Lauren.
The illustrations were done in ink.

Candlewick Press
99 Dover Street
Somerville, Massachusetts 02144

www.candlewick.com

To my mother with love
A

To Peter Tobia,
aka Grandad
LT

Anna Goes to Canada

Anna Hibiscus lives in Africa. Amazing Africa. In a country called Nigeria. She lives with her grandmother and her grandfather; her mother and her father; her aunties and her uncles; her many, many cousins; and her two baby brothers, Double and Trouble.

But now Anna Hibiscus is going far overseas.

“Is her suitcase in the car?” Grandfather asked.

“What about her photo album?” called Grandmother, hurrying over.

“Anna Hibiscus, are you ready?” shouted Uncle Tunde, standing by the car.

Anna Hibiscus came out of the house, holding her mother’s hand.

“Do you have the book we wrote your stories in?” shouted cousin Clarity.

“What about your phone money?” asked Anna Hibiscus’s father.

“Is your camera safe?” asked Uncle Eldest.

Anna Hibiscus nodded and nodded. She had her photo album and her book and her phone money and her camera in her new handbag. And in her suitcase was the surprise present from her mother and the beautiful new warm red suit and the empty pot to bring back snow for Double and Trouble.

Anna Hibiscus was going to Canada. Today. Now! She was leaving her entire family and the big white house for one whole month.

Grandfather held up his hand. "Anna Hibiscus!" he said loudly. At once everybody was quiet. "Do not forget what I have told you!" Grandfather said.

Anna Hibiscus nodded again. Grandfather had told her many things. "Be good, Anna Hibiscus. And have fun. But remember, do not go near any dogs. People in cold countries allow dogs into their houses. This is because they do not live together with the whole of their family as we do here. Instead they have dogs for company."

"Yes, Grandfather," Anna Hibiscus said seriously.

Grandfather had been telling her the same thing since her tickets to Canada had come. But Anna Hibiscus was sure that he was wrong. Nobody would allow a dog into their house. Dogs live in packs and eat garbage and bite people. They are thin and angry and have worms.

"Granny Canada will look after you," Grandfather concluded hopefully. "She will not allow you to enter any house that contains a dog. Of that I am sure."

Anna Hibiscus's mother looked as though she was about to say something. Then Double and Trouble started to cry.

Quickly Anna's father put Anna into Uncle Tunde's car. Her mother jumped in beside her. But too late. Everybody had joined Double Trouble in crying. Chocolate and Angel were the first. Then the aunties started loudly. It was so sad to say goodbye.

"Go! Go!" said Grandmother, dabbing her eyes.

Uncle Tunde started the engine.

"Goodbye, Anna!" sobbed Chocolate and Angel.

"Don't forget us!" wailed Benz and Wonderful.

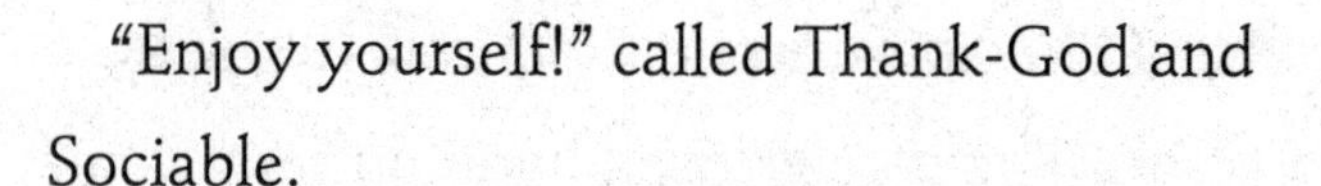

"Enjoy yourself!" called Thank-God and Sociable.

"Write about everything!" wept Clarity and Joy and Common Sense.

"Be careful!" sniffed Auntie Joly.

"Don't forget to snap many photos!" called Uncle Eldest and Uncle Habibi.

"Come back soon!" sobbed Grandmother and Grandfather.

"Come soon! Come soon!" wailed Double and Trouble.

And they were off.

Anna Hibiscus turned around in her seat to wave. The gates closed behind them. The big white house where Anna Hibiscus had lived all her life was gone.

They turned the corner. The white walls around the garden were gone too.

A big lump came into Anna Hibiscus's throat.

Anna's mother put her arm around her. "Don't worry, Anna," she whispered.

But Anna did worry. She worried all the way to the airport.

The airport was big. Big enough for airplanes to land inside. There were many, many people running around like ants who had lost their way.

But Anna Hibiscus's father knew exactly where to go. He held Anna's suitcase and headed across the enormous floor in one purposeful direction. Maybe it was the suitcase that knew what to do. It had waited so many years to travel. Now it was eager and ready to go. And Uncle Tunde and Anna's mother and Anna Hibiscus all followed.

Anna Hibiscus's father stopped at a little open office. A lady checked the things he gave her. Passport. Ticket.

"They are all correct," she said. "Now, who else is traveling?"

"Just Anna Hibiscus," said her father.

The lady looked at Anna Hibiscus. Then she said, "She is too small. Too small to go alone."

Just then a voice from behind them shouted, "*Femi! Tunde! Emily!* What are you all doing here?"

They all turned around. A big lady was standing there, smiling at them. "Auntie Jumoke!" shouted Anna's father, and threw his arms around the big lady.

Anna Hibiscus's mother bent her knee to the auntie, who shook her hand warmly.

"Auntie Jum-Jum!" Uncle Tunde laughed. "What are you doing here?"

"I am traveling," said the big auntie. "Aren't I always traveling?"

She sighed and shook her head. "Ten children and thirty-four grandchildren and all of them scattered around the world."

She looked down at Anna Hibiscus. Then she looked up at Anna Hibiscus's mother and father. "Is this Anna Hibiscus, who gives clothes to poor children?"

Anna Hibiscus's mother and father nodded.

"She is on her way to Canada to visit my mother," said Anna's mother.

"You are like me," sighed the auntie, patting Anna's head. "Family scattered all over the world."

The lady in the office interrupted. "Is this child traveling alone?" she asked again, loud and irritated.

"Of course not!" replied the big auntie. "We are going together!"

And she said to the lady in the office, "This is my second cousin's granddaughter." Which was true.

The big auntie, Auntie Jumoke, arranged for her seat on the airplane to be next to Anna Hibiscus's seat, and together they watched their suitcases disappear.

Then Anna Hibiscus kissed and hugged her mother and her father and Uncle Tunde, and her mother and father again, and her mother again. Then she started to cry.

"Come here, poor child," said Auntie Jumoke, picking up Anna Hibiscus along with her own seven items of hand luggage. "Before you can say hello to them again, you must first say goodbye."

Then the big auntie, with Anna Hibiscus in her arms, walked around the corner toward the airplane, where only the passengers could go.

"Have fun, Anna Hibiscus!" shouted Uncle Tunde.

When they were seated on the plane, Auntie Jumoke showed Anna Hibiscus how to fasten her seat belt. She gave her advice on the toilets.

"Only go when it is pressing," she said. "It is not a place you want to visit too often. But do not wait until it is *too* late because there is often a queue. People are so slow!"

Then the plane took off. It carried Anna Hibiscus away from Nigeria and the beautiful city of Lagos and her whole family.

Anna Hibiscus held her handbag tight to stop herself from being frightened. Her hands closed around something square and hard. The photo album that Grandmother had made for her!

Anna opened the photo album and started to cry. She wanted to see her family. She wanted to go home.

Auntie Jumoke leaned over her shoulder. She pointed at a photo of Anna Hibiscus's father.

"That boy," she sighed. "I remember one day I asked him to catch my young rooster. He chased it up and down the compound, up and down. Eventually the rooster flew up onto my roof. Your father followed him up there. The rooster flew down. Your father could not. He had to remain there until we sent someone to the next village to borrow a ladder."

Anna Hibiscus stopped crying and started to laugh. Before she stopped laughing, Auntie Jumoke told her another story. This time about Auntie Joly.

"I sent that girl to the river to wash clothes one day. At her own house she was used to washing at the tap. She scrubbed the clothes on a rock, but when it came time to rinse, she tipped the whole bucket of clothes into the water. The river carried the clothes away, and your auntie started to scream and cry. At last a fisherman caught them in his nets and brought them back to me."

Anna Hibiscus could not stop laughing at all the silly things her father and aunties and her uncles and even Grandmother and Grandfather used to do.

Anna Hibiscus laughed all the way across Africa. A lady came along with trays of food. Anna Hibiscus's stomach rumbled. But Auntie Jumoke waved the trays away.

"That is not food," Auntie Jumoke said. "It is plastic, pretending to be food. Only oyinbos from foreign countries can digest that sort of thing."

Anna was worried again. Last night she had eaten as much of Uncle Bizi Sunday's good African food as she could squeeze into her belly. She had been sure that she would not be hungry again for a whole month and that she would not have to eat oyinbo food. But she was hungry again already!

Auntie Jumoke was looking in her hand luggage. She pulled out old ice-cream boxes filled with fried chicken and jollof rice and moi-moi.

"Wa jeun!" she said. "Let's eat!"

Suddenly Anna Hibiscus remembered the yummy food that Uncle Bizi Sunday had packed in her suitcase for her. She would not have to eat oyinbo food after all.

Anna Hibiscus smiled happily and shared Auntie Jumoke's food. She ate and ate and ate. Then she fell asleep.

When she woke up, the plane was landing in Canada.

Anna Hibiscus stepped out. It was *so* cold. For a moment, Anna Hibiscus's lungs forgot how to breathe!

Anna's eyes opened wide. But there was nothing to see! The cold had sucked all the color out of Canada. Just as it had sucked the breath out of Anna. Canada was only white and gray.

Anna Hibiscus followed Auntie Jumoke through passport control. Then Auntie Jumoke showed Anna where to find her suitcase. They walked to where Granny Canada and all the other passengers' friends and relatives would be waiting.

Auntie Jumoke was swallowed up by her own family, and Anna Hibiscus stood alone in front of a sea of white faces. She had never imagined that there were so many white faces in the world.

A soft voice said,
"Hello, Anna Hibiscus."

Anna Hibiscus looked up. An old lady who looked just like Granny Canada in her photo stood there.

She put her arms around Anna Hibiscus. And her neck smelled like Anna's mother's neck! Exactly the same! "Hello, Granny Canada," Anna Hibiscus said.

"Hello, Anna Hibiscus," said Granny Canada. "I am glad you are here at last!"

Anna Hibiscus looked down. She wanted to say she was glad too, but she was thinking of dogs and plastic food and cold that sucks away breath. She was thinking of her whole family and the big white house so far away. So she said nothing.

"Are you ready to see snow?" Granny Canada asked gently.

Anna Hibiscus nodded. But she still looked down.

Granny Canada took a big warm red coat out of her bag. She put it on Anna Hibiscus. It was just Anna's size. Anna was surprised. Then she put a warm fluffy pink hat on Anna. Then she knelt down and took off Anna's sandals and put big furry boots onto her feet. They fit perfectly. She slipped soft pink gloves onto Anna's hands. Anna Hibiscus smiled at Granny Canada. She was so surprised. And warm.

Then Granny Canada took Anna's suitcase and Anna Hibiscus followed her out of the airport.

The snow was falling thick and white and bright. The night sky was black. The moon shone on each flake. Anna Hibiscus looked up. Her eyes shone and her mouth opened wide.

"Isn't it lovely?" Granny Canada asked.

Snowflakes landed on Anna Hibiscus's face. Anna Hibiscus nodded. It was lovely. A snowflake landed on her nose. Anna Hibiscus laughed. Then she knew. She was glad to be here too.

Anna Hibiscus started to sing. First her heart and then her mouth joined in.

"Snow, you are so wonderful,
I am glad to tell you so.
Snow, you are so sweet-o,
I am glad to taste you-o.
Snow, you are wonderful,
I am glad to see you so!"

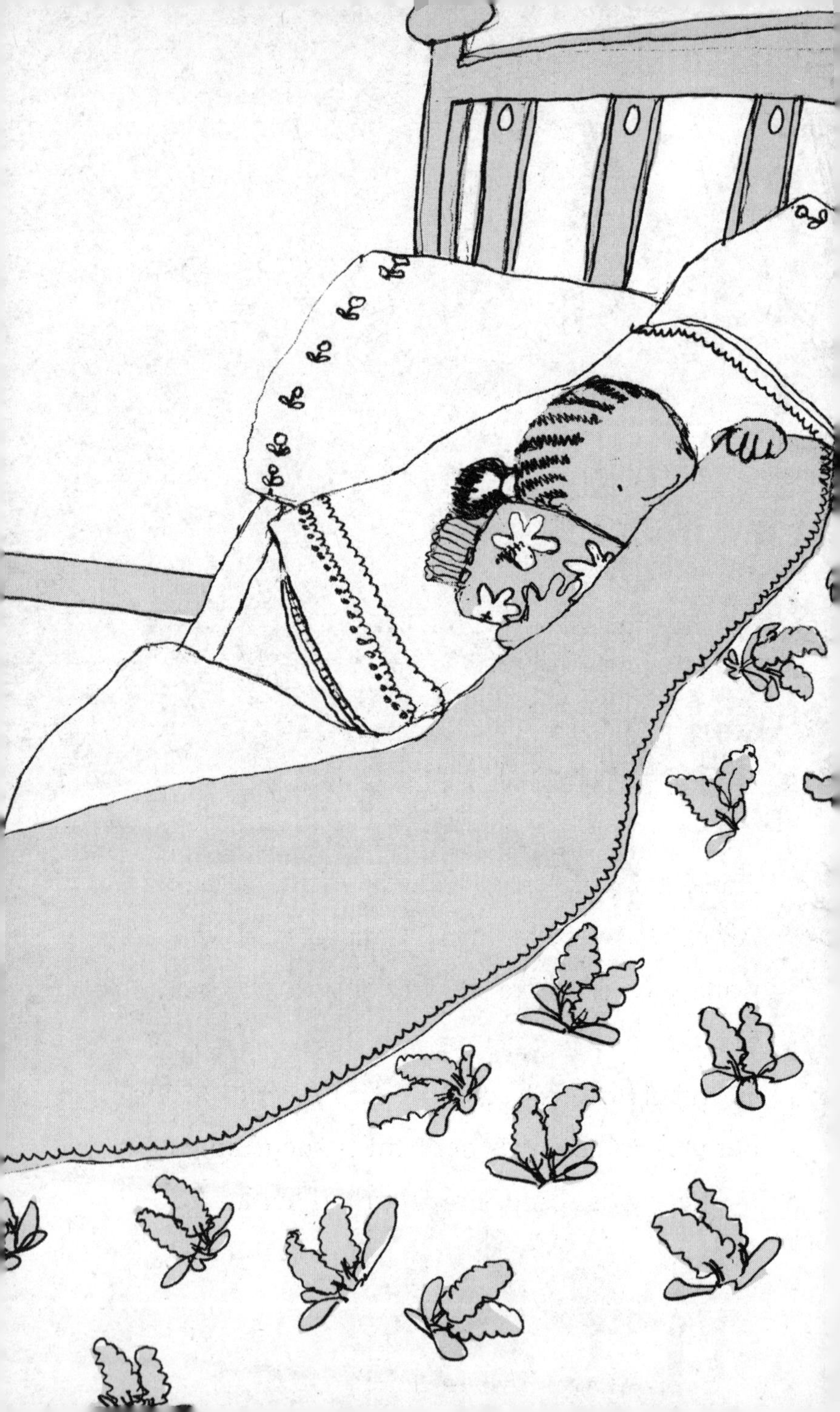

Anna's First Day

Anna Hibiscus was in Canada. Africa, amazing Africa, was very far away. Canada, cold Canada, was where she was now. It was her first day.

Anna Hibiscus woke up. The sheet covering her was so heavy. Where am I? she thought.

There was something warm in her arms.

Anna Hibiscus squeezed it. It was soft. She remembered a hot-water bottle covered with knitted hibiscus flowers. A surprise from her mother.

Her nose was cold. And suddenly Anna Hibiscus remembered where she was! Canada!

Anna jumped straight out of bed. She ran across the cold floor and looked out the window.

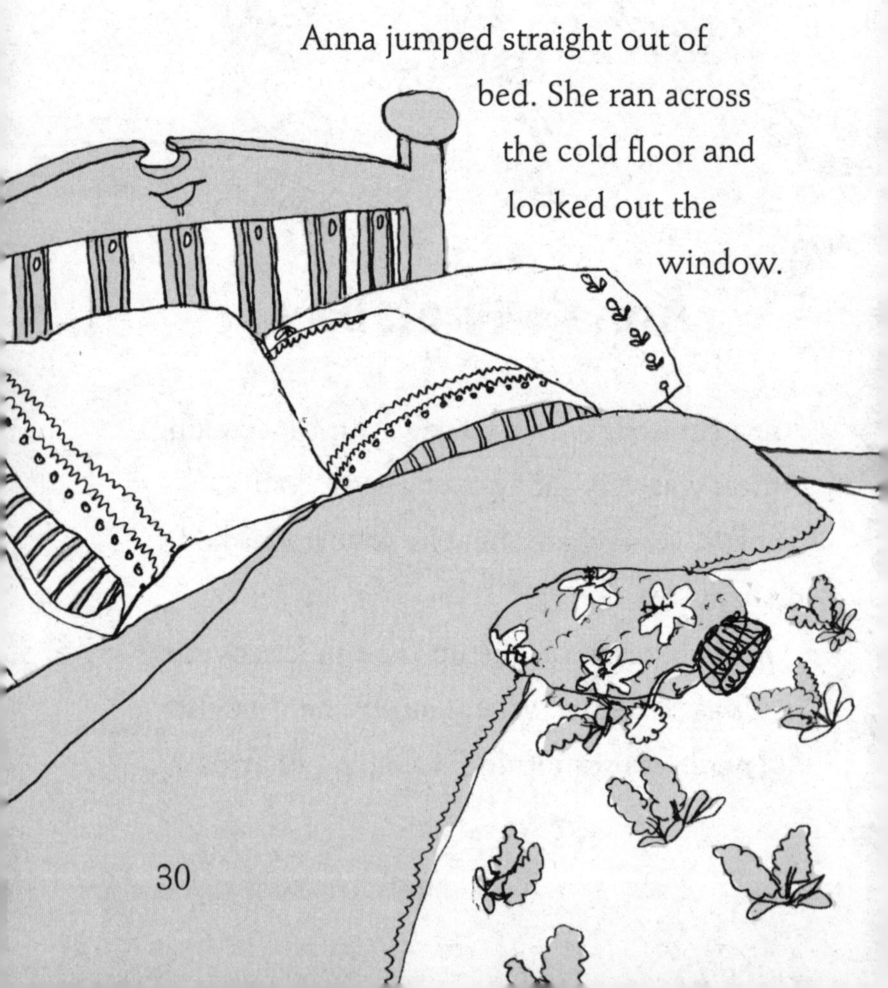

Snow! Snow! Nothing but snow! Anna Hibiscus sighed happily.

She turned around to tell her cousins. But there was nobody there. Only an empty bed piled high with blankets and quilts and a lonely pink hot-water bottle.

Anna Hibiscus was alone. For the first time in her life, she had woken up alone.

There was a knock on the door. Anna Hibiscus rushed to open it. It was Granny Canada. And a dog. A big white dog with sharp pointed teeth who jumped into the room.

Anna Hibiscus closed her eyes and screamed.

"Qimmiq!" said Granny Canada's voice. "Down! Out!"

Anna Hibiscus heard the door shut. The dog was gone.

"Anna?" said Granny Canada's soft voice. "I'm sorry. I did not know that you were afraid of dogs."

Anna Hibiscus did not say anything. Everybody was afraid of dogs.

"Her name is Qimmiq," said Granny Canada. "I have had her all her life and she has never, ever hurt anybody."

Anna Hibiscus still said nothing. Dogs have worms and germs and they like to bite people.

"Anna Hibiscus," said Granny Canada, "Qimmiq only wants to be your friend."

Anna Hibiscus could never be friends with a dog. Anna Hibiscus's heart made a miserable noise.

From behind the door came exactly the same noise. Anna opened her eyes in surprise.

"It is Qimmiq," said Granny Canada. "She is miserable. She does not understand why she is shut out alone."

Anna Hibiscus was so surprised. She kept her eyes open wide.

"Let us unpack your suitcase and get you dressed," said Granny Canada. "You must be cold."

So Anna Hibiscus unpacked socks and pants and undershirts and her two long-sleeved dresses. Then she watched in surprise as Granny Canada opened drawers and brought out long yellow socks that went right up and turned into underwear.

"Tights," said Granny Canada.

Granny Canada also brought out a yellow long-sleeved T-shirt and a thick blue long-sleeved T-shirt and a knitted cardigan and thick padded blue trousers.

Anna Hibiscus looked at the pile of clothes. Was she supposed to wear all of those? At once? "Come on," said Granny Canada.

So Anna Hibiscus put on her underpants and her undershirt. What was supposed to go on next? Granny Canada passed Anna

Hibiscus the long-sleeved T-shirt. Anna pulled it on.

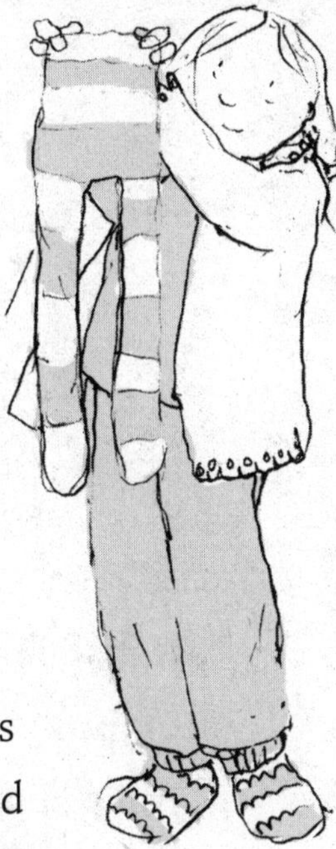

Granny Canada held out the tights. Anna Hibiscus looked at them. She had never worn anything like them before.

"This way round," Granny Canada said.

Anna Hibiscus sat on the bed and put one of her feet slowly into the tights.

"That's it," said Granny Canada. "Slowly, or the legs will get twisted."

Anna Hibiscus's foot got stuck. She pushed it. But the tights would not let her foot go in any farther. Granny Canada bent over and pulled the tights out straight.

"Try now," she said.

Anna Hibiscus pushed her foot harder, and this time her foot shot all the way down the tights so hard and so fast that Granny Canada fell over backward in surprise.

Anna Hibiscus jumped up to help Granny Canada. But she forgot that she had only one foot in the tights. Anna Hibiscus fell down next to Granny Canada.

Granny Canada laughed and laughed. She could not stop. Anna Hibiscus started to laugh too.

At last Granny Canada took a handkerchief out of her pocket and wiped her eyes. "Let's start again," she said.

She took the tangled leg of the tights and bunched it up open so that Anna Hibiscus could fit her other foot straight into the foot of the tights. Granny Canada pulled the tights all the way up Anna Hibiscus's legs to her waist.

"I think it is safe to get up now," she said.

Anna Hibiscus got up. She looked down at her legs. They were yellow. They were so yellow that they did a little yellow dance. Anna Hibiscus was surprised. She did not know that her legs would like being yellow so much.

Granny Canada smiled. She passed Anna Hibiscus the rest of the clothes, and after a lot of wriggling and pushing and straightening and pulling, Anna Hibiscus was in!

"Breakfast?" asked Granny Canada.

Anna Hibiscus's stomach rumbled in reply.

"Coming?" asked Granny Canada with her hand on the door.

Anna Hibiscus did not answer. She did not move. Then she said, "Dogs have germs and they like to bite people."

"Not all dogs," said Granny Canada. "Have you ever been bitten by a dog?"

Anna Hibiscus shook her head.

"I have never been near to a dog to let it bite me," she said.

"You have never been near a dog?" asked Granny Canada in surprise.

Anna Hibiscus shook her head.

"Never petted a dog?"

Anna Hibiscus shook her head hard.

"Don't you have friends who have dogs?" asked Granny Canada.

"No," said Anna Hibiscus. "Dogs live outside and eat rubbish. They are dirty.

People chase them away so that they don't bite children or bring sickness."

"Oh," said Granny Canada.

Granny Canada went out and shut the dog in another room. Then Anna Hibiscus came out and followed Granny Canada to the kitchen.

Anna Hibiscus looked around the room in surprise. There were cupboards and a sink and a fridge, and there was also a sofa and armchairs and a table in the middle. It was not just a kitchen! It was a kitchen-living-dining room.

Anna had never seen one of these before!

Granny Canada opened cupboards and started putting things on the table. Anna Hibiscus remembered what Auntie Jumoke had said about plastic food.

Anna Hibiscus ran down the hallway and back to her own room. When Granny Canada turned around, Anna Hibiscus was sitting at the table surrounded by the yummy spicy food that Uncle Bizi Sunday had packed up for her.

"That looks good," said Granny Canada. "Shall I put the chocolate cereal away?"

Chocolate cereal! Anna Hibiscus's eyes opened wide. Once Auntie Comfort had brought cereal from America for the cousins. But not chocolate cereal!

Anna Hibiscus looked at Uncle Bizi Sunday's food. She could eat it anytime. She could eat some for lunch!

"Chocolate cereal for breakfast, I think!" Anna Hibiscus said.

She wished that her cousins were here to share this. Anna could not wait to phone and tell them all about it. Thinking about her cousins made her feel sad. But she could not phone now. They would still be asleep.

So after breakfast, to cheer herself up, Anna Hibiscus read to Granny Canada from the book where her cousins had written down all her adventures. Granny Canada loved the bit where Anna sold oranges on the street. She loved the bit where Double and Trouble ate all the sweets.

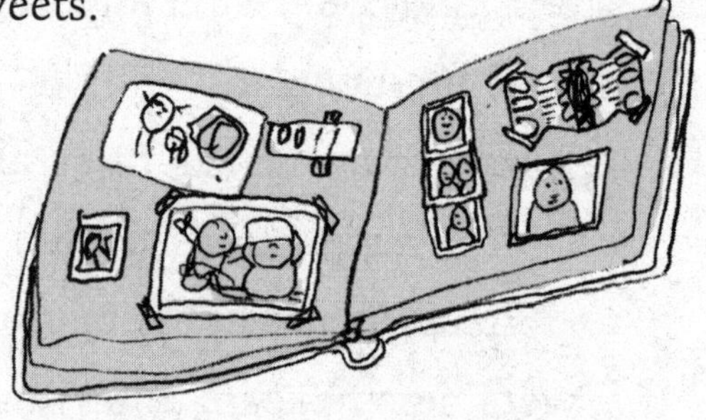

Anna Hibiscus showed Granny Canada the photos in her album of everybody in her stories. That made her feel sad again. A tear dripped off Anna's nose. Then the dog barked.

"You are missing them," said Granny Canada. "And Qimmiq is missing me."

Anna Hibiscus was so surprised, she stopped crying.

Granny Canada took down her big photo album and showed Anna the photos.

"Who is this in the snow?" Anna Hibiscus asked, pointing at a brown photograph of a small man surrounded by snow.

"That is your great-great-grandfather," said Granny Canada. "His smile reminds me of someone . . ."

"My great-great-grandfather?" said Anna Hibiscus. She had forgotten that Granny Canada's family was her family too.

"Yes," said Granny Canada. "He spent all his winters out on the snow and sea ice."

Wow! thought Anna Hibiscus. Maybe that was why she loved snow so much. Because she had a snow family too.

"He loved snow," said Granny Canada. "But one day he almost died out on the ice."

"How did he almost die?" asked Anna Hibiscus.

"He was hunting a seal when he fell through the ice and into the frozen sea."

"What happened?" asked Anna Hibiscus.

Granny Canada smiled. "Luckily someone else was there and he was rescued."

"How?" asked Anna.

"He was pulled out of the hole in the ice," said Granny Canada. "Someone risked their own life to save him."

"Who?" gasped Anna Hibiscus.

"His favorite dog," said Granny Canada.

"His dog!" Anna Hibiscus was shocked.

"Oh yes," said Granny Canada. "He had many dogs. They pulled his sled and helped him hunt food. Our family could not have survived out on the snow without dogs. And this one saved him from certain death."

"From certain death!" gasped Anna Hibiscus.

Granny Canada pointed to a photo of a big white dog with white pointed teeth.

"If the first Qimmiq had not saved your grandfather, I would not have been born," said Granny Canada. "Nor would your mother."

"Oh," said Anna Hibiscus. Then she thought, Nor me. I would not have been born either.

Granny Canada said, "Time for a walk. Let us go and see the snow we love. Qimmiq must come. She needs exercise."

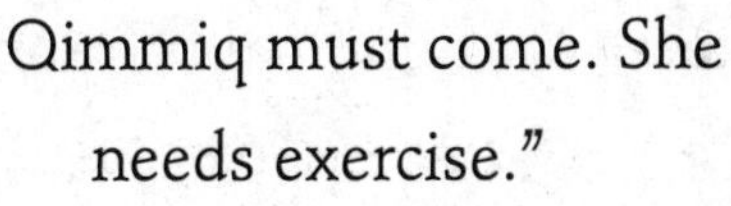

So Anna Hibiscus and Granny Canada and Qimmiq went for a walk in the snow. Granny Canada kept Qimmiq on a strong leash. Anna Hibiscus stayed well away from her big teeth. But she looked at her out of the corner of her eye.

"She is the many times granddaughter of the first Qimmiq," said Granny Canada.

"Oh!" said Anna Hibiscus again. Then she stopped looking at Qimmiq and looked at the snow instead.

Heaps of snow! Banks of snow! Fields of snow!

Out of a snowdrift, a chimney was pouring smoke. Anna Hibiscus laughed

out loud. That was not a snowdrift! That was a house!

Anna Hibiscus took photos of the snow with the camera her uncles had given her. She took lots of the snowdrift chimney and laughed again.

Then Granny Canada took photos of Anna in the snow. Anna ran across the snow. It was crunchy and hard. She made snowballs. She and Granny Canada made snow angels. They made a snowman.

"Time to go in now, Anna Hibiscus," said Granny Canada.

But Anna Hibiscus was running on the snow, listening to the *crunch*, *crunch*, *crunch*. She wanted to run forever across the bright and shiny snow and never stop.

"Come on, Anna," called Granny Canada, "before you get too cold!"

But Anna Hibiscus did not hear. She was climbing up a snowdrift now.

Suddenly Anna Hibiscus disappeared headfirst into the snowdrift.

"Anna!" shouted Granny Canada, and let go of Qimmiq's leash.

Deep in the snowdrift, Anna Hibiscus struggled. The more she moved, the deeper she fell. The snow was heavy on her arms and legs and on the back of her head. Anna Hibiscus could not breathe.

I am going to die, she thought.

Somebody caught hold of Anna Hibiscus's foot and pulled hard. They pulled her out of the snowdrift and up into the air. Anna Hibiscus lay on the ground and breathed. The air was cold, but it was so lovely to breathe.

Anna Hibiscus looked up. There was nobody there. Nobody except Qimmiq. She was sitting quietly with her head on one side, looking at Anna with worried eyes.

Granny Canada arrived, running, and caught Anna Hibiscus up in her arms and hugged her.

"Are you OK?" Granny asked.

"She saved me! She saved me!" Anna Hibiscus cried. "Just like Great-Great-Grandfather! She saved me from certain death!"

Anna Hibiscus stopped hugging Granny Canada. She looked at Qimmiq and smiled. Then she very carefully stroked the big white dog.

"Thank you for saving me," Anna Hibiscus said. Then she smiled and she smiled.

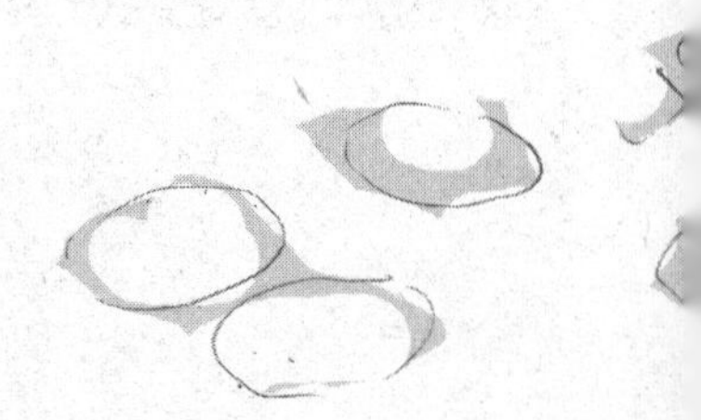

And suddenly Granny Canada realized exactly who Great-Great-Grandfather's smile reminded her of.

Why, Anna Hibiscus, of course!

Canada is full of ice and snow. Ice is cold. Snow is cold. Especially when I fell all the way into it. But Canada is COZY too. Cozy means warm and safe and happy. Granny Canada's kitchen is cozy. Good dogs like Qimmiq are cozy.

Anna was writing. And thinking . . . that there was one big *c* word that Canada was not. And that was *cousins*. Canada did not mean cousins.

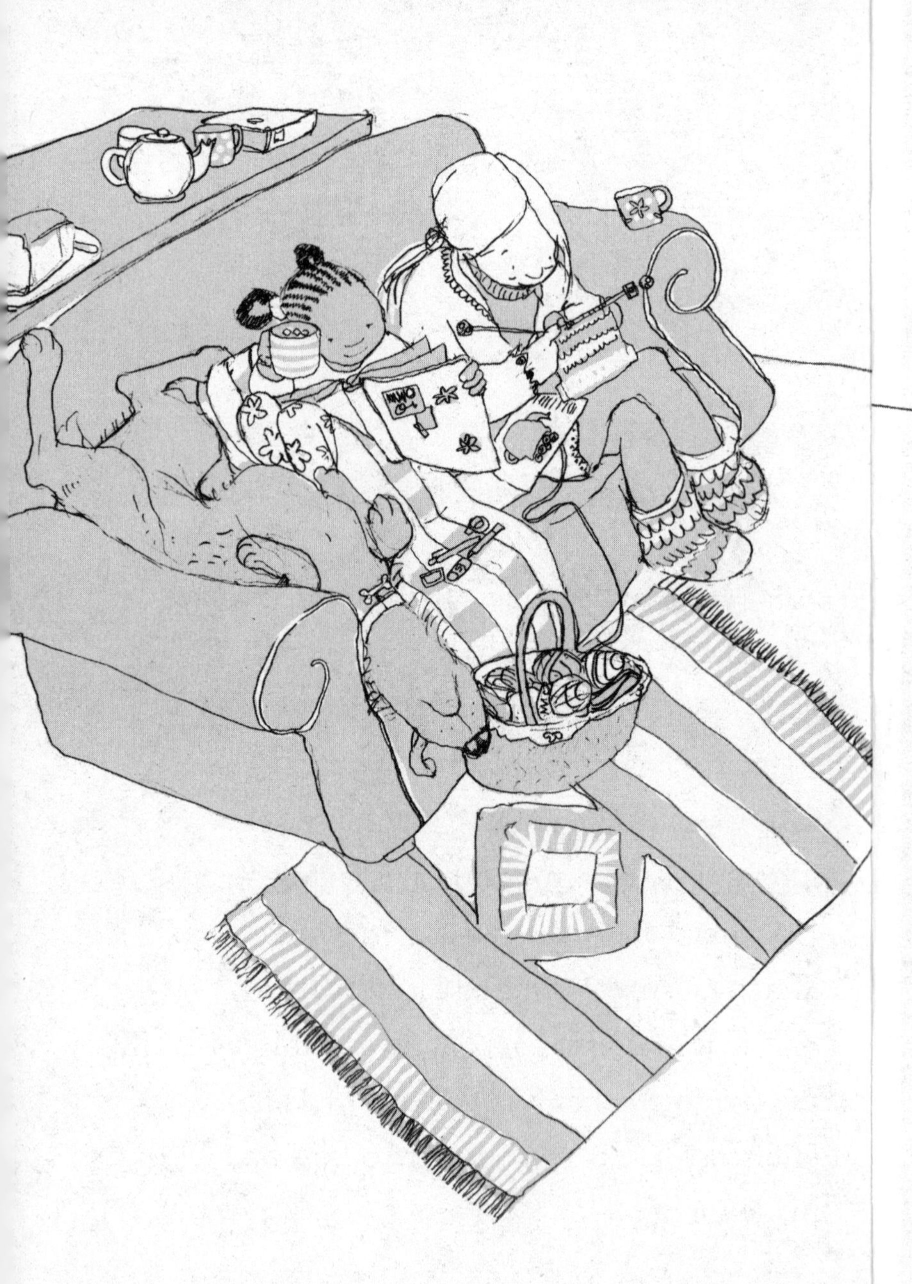

Cousins or Friends?

Anna Hibiscus was in Canada. Cold, cold Canada. Africa, amazing Africa, was far, far away. But Canada was amazing too.

Anna Hibiscus was sitting in Granny Canada's kitchen-living-dining room. Qimmiq was warm and heavy on her feet. Hot chocolate was steaming under her nose. Granny Canada's knitting needles were *clack-clack-clacking* happily. Anna Hibiscus was writing in her "Adventures of Anna Hibiscus" book. The one her cousins had made for her.

Anna Hibiscus missed her cousins. She could not stop missing them.

Anna wanted Benz and Wonderful to eat chocolate cereal with her every single morning. She wanted to jump into her big hot baths with Chocolate and Angel.

Anna wanted Clarity and Joy and Common Sense to walk with her around the big bright shiny shops that sold every single thing in the world! She wanted Miracle and Sweetheart to hear all the new stories that Granny Canada knew.

Suddenly Anna Hibiscus stopped writing and thinking. She had heard something. Something outside. Anna Hibiscus ran to the window.

"Look! Look! Look!" she shouted.

Qimmiq jumped up at the window. She wagged her tail fast.

Children had stopped outside Granny Canada's gate. They looked like they were going somewhere, carrying big bright plastic bowls and boards.

Quick, quick! Anna Hibiscus fought her way into her snowsuit and her hat and her gloves.

Anna Hibiscus rushed out into Granny Canada's yard with Qimmiq barking beside her.

"Hello!" Anna Hibiscus shouted.

All the children turned to look at Anna Hibiscus.

One boy said, "We were thinking of ringing your bell."

A big girl with freckles said, "Do you want to play?"

"Oh yes!" said Anna Hibiscus. She was so happy.

Anna looked up at the house. Granny Canada was waving. "Go and play!" she shouted, smiling.

"Cool!" said the big girl.

"Cool!" said the big boy.

"Cool?" asked Anna Hibiscus.

"Come on!" shouted all the children.

The children started to run down the road, laughing and carrying their big plastic bowls and boards.

Anna Hibiscus and Qimmiq followed, Qimmiq's head bumping on Anna's hand.

They ran out of the town to a steep bumpy slope and a frozen lake. There was not one single footprint in the shining white snow. The lake was smooth. The trees all around it dangled sparkling icicles. The mountains rose up behind them, strong and watchful. And some ravens were there too, black against the blue sky, waving their long feathers.

Anna Hibiscus took a deep happy breath.

She watched the other children drop their boards and bowls and run shouting and shrieking down the slope to the lake. Anna Hibiscus followed. At the bottom, one of the girls gave Anna Hibiscus some boots. The boots had metal on the bottom. Anna Hibiscus recognized them. Skates! This lake must be safe for skating on!

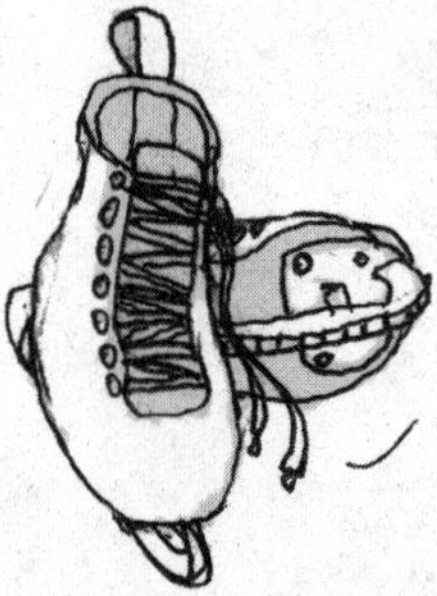

"I brought them for you," said the girl shyly. "They used to be mine. Will you be my friend? I never had a friend from Africa before."

Anna Hibiscus did not know whether to say yes or no. Did the girl want to be her friend only because she was from Africa? So Anna just put on the skates. She had seen so many photographs of her mother skating. Anna Hibiscus wanted to skate too. It looked just like flying!

Anna Hibiscus stood up on the ice and fell down on her face. Ow! Everybody laughed!

The girl who wanted to be her friend tried to pull her up, but Anna slipped again and pulled the girl over with her. Ow! Ow!

The other children laughed even harder.

The girl got up and skated away. She did not want to be laughed at too.

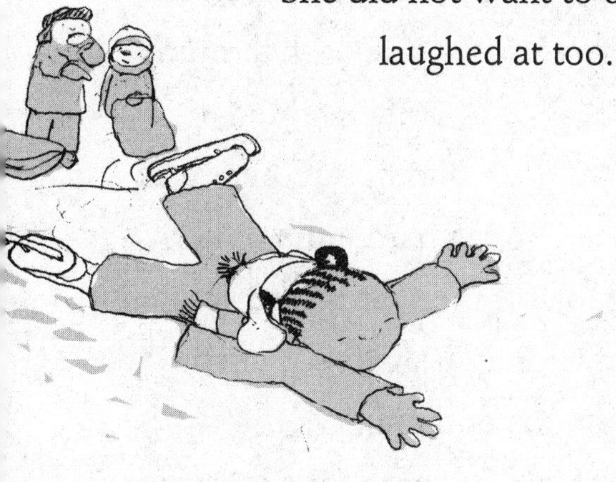

Anna watched her go. So that girl did not really want to be Anna's friend after all. But Anna Hibiscus was not going to give up. She could learn to skate on her own.

A rude-looking boy skated close to Anna.

"You can't skate because you are African," he said.

Anna Hibiscus sat down on the ice with a thump. She wanted to shout, but there was a big hard lump in her throat. She took off the skates. She wanted to go back to Granny Canada's. But she did not know how to get there.

The other children skated for a long time. When they were finished, Anna followed them back up the slope toward the town. They were all talking to each other and laughing. Nobody spoke to her. Anna Hibiscus was glad to be going home.

But when the children got to the top of the slope, they picked up the bowls and boards they had left there and turned to face the lake again.

One by one and two by two, they got onto their boards and slid down the snowy slope. Faster and faster they went—until they hit a big bump in the snow and the plastic slides bounced up and everybody fell off.

Nobody reached the bottom.

Anna Hibiscus and Qimmiq watched and watched.

Anna could not take her eyes off the snow slides. She forgot everything else.

"Do you want to have a go?" a small voice asked. It was the same girl who had lent Anna her old skates. Now she was holding out her snow slide.

"Yes," said Anna without taking her eyes off the snow.

She took the snow slide. She looked down the slope. Anna Hibiscus got onto the slide.

"Does anyone want to take her down?" called the big girl with freckles.

But nobody did. They had all seen how badly Anna Hibiscus skated. Who would want to go on a snow slide with her?

Anna Hibiscus was glad. She wanted to be alone, skimming down the slope. Unless . . .

Anna Hibiscus looked at Qimmiq. Qimmiq jumped onto the slide with Anna. The children laughed. Anna Hibiscus did not care.

She was off!
Anna Hibiscus could hear the snow crunch under her slide. Somehow she knew which way to lean over every bump so that she soared through the air. She was flying!

Anna Hibiscus flew all the way down to the bottom of the slope without falling off once!

At the bottom, Anna Hibiscus laughed.
Qimmiq rolled around in the snow, barking.

Then Anna Hibiscus heard shouting. All the children were running and shrieking down the slope toward her.

Anna Hibiscus watched them. She did not smile.

"That was so cool!" yelled the boys.

"So cool!" they all shouted.

"How did you do that?" asked the big girl.

The rude boy was the last one to arrive. "Africans can't do that!" he shouted.

Anna Hibiscus wished that Grandmother was here to say a thing or two to that boy. But she was in Nigeria. Anna Hibiscus was alone. And she knew that if she did not say something now, she would feel ashamed.

So Anna Hibiscus looked the children in the eye.

"My name is Anna Hibiscus," said Anna. "I could not skate because it was my first time. Not because I am African."

The rude boy's face went red, and he looked at the ground.

Anna said, "I don't know why I am good at snow sliding. I just am. Because I am Anna."

One of the girls looked like she was going to say something.

But Anna said quickly, "I only want to be friends with people who want to be friends with me because I am Anna. Not because I am African."

Then Anna Hibiscus stopped talking. Her throat felt dry.

Some of the other children were looking at her, and some were looking down at the snow. None of them said anything now.

Anna started to trudge up the slope alone with Qimmiq. She was going to go back now. Even if she got lost.

Before she got to the top, a voice shouted, “Stop!”

Anna Hibiscus turned around. The children were following her up.

“We are sorry, Anna Hibiscus,” said one of the big girls.

“Really sorry,” said one of the little boys.

“We did not know it was your first time skating,” said another girl. “Honestly.”

Anna Hibiscus took a deep breath.

"OK," she said.

"How come it was your first time?" asked a little girl. "What do you do in the winter in Africa?"

"We don't have winter in Africa," said Anna Hibiscus.

"No winter!" the rude boy shouted. "No snow? No ice? Not at all?"

Anna Hibiscus shook her head.

"So what do you have?" he asked.

"We have the harmattan," said Anna Hibiscus, "and the rainy season."

"What's that?" asked a girl.

Anna Hibiscus explained about the harmattan wind blowing sand from the Sahara Desert all the way across West Africa. And she explained about the rainy season, when it rains for six months and the roads flood and turn to mud.

"Cool!" said one of the girls.

"Wow!" said a big boy.

Anna Hibiscus stopped talking. She did not tell them about the big white house or about Grandmother and Grandfather and her cousins and the mango trees and the chickens. She did not tell them about Double and Trouble, her brothers.

She did not know if she liked them yet.

Then one of the big boys said, “Do you want to use my sled, Anna Hibiscus?”

“Go on, Anna,” said one of the big girls. “His sled has never made it all the way down before.”

“Yeah,” said another boy. “You’d be doing it a favor!”

Anna Hibiscus smiled. She took the big board the boy was holding out. Anna and Qimmiq got on.

There was room for more children. Anna Hibiscus looked over her shoulder. "Taxi!" she shouted.

The children laughed. Two of them jumped on.

"I'm Lauren!" shouted one of them.

"I'm Cara!" shouted the other.

And off they flew!

Anna Hibiscus spent the rest of the day flying down the slope with Cara and Lauren and Tessa and Rosie and Tom and Steve and Joe and Mark.

"I was wrong, Anna Hibiscus," said Tom, the rude boy, as they walked home. "Africans are cool."

Soon they were at Granny Canada's gate.

"See you tomorrow!" everybody shouted.

"We'll come and get you," said Cara.

"We'll bring our sleds," said Tom.

"And our skates!" said Lauren.

Everybody laughed.

"Do you *want* to play with us again tomorrow?" Rosie asked.

"Yes!" said Anna Hibiscus. "Definitely."

"Cool!" shouted all the children.

"Canada is so cool!" Anna Hibiscus told Grandfather that night on the phone.

"Don't you mean cold?" his voice crackled.

"Let me hear her," Anna heard Grandmother's voice say.

"Canada is cool," Anna told Grandmother.

"She means cold," Grandmother's voice said to Grandfather.

"There are no cousins here," Anna told Angel and Clarity and Benz.

"But I have got friends," she told her mother.

"Friends?" asked Double.

"Friends!" said Anna Hibiscus. "They are not so kind as cousins. Not so brilliant as brothers. But they are cool. Friends are definitely cool!"

Anna's Christmas in Canada

Anna Hibiscus was in Canada. Cold, cozy, cool Canada!

It was Christmas Eve. Anna Hibiscus was in the kitchen-living-dining room with Granny Canada. She had been there for days. Mixing butter and sugar. Sifting flour and baking powder. Beating eggs and cream. Measuring cinnamon and nutmeg and ginger. Stirring in cherries and raisins and currants. Melting chocolate and molasses.

Can you guess what she was making?

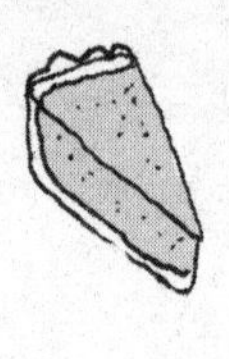

Sweet pastries and mince pies, rich fruitcakes and chocolate

Yule logs, pumpkin pies and trifle, eggnog and gingerbread houses. Christmas food, of course!

Anna Hibiscus had never tasted Canadian Christmas food before. She had heard about it from her mother. She had wondered what it tasted like.

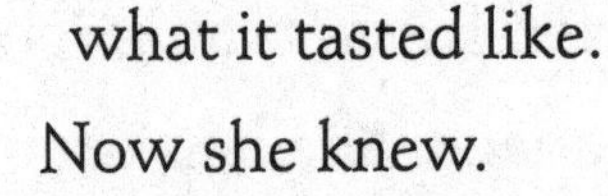

Now she knew.

It tasted like heaven.

Sweet and creamy and rich and . . . heavenly!

Anna Hibiscus stopped stirring and mixing and beating for a second.

At home in the big white compound in Nigeria, the goats and chickens would be fattening. Uncle Bizi Sunday would be frying a mountain of rice and crayfish. Bean curd moi-moi wrapped in plantain leaves would be boiling in oil drums.

Aunties would be pounding, pounding, pounding creamy yams. Anna Hibiscus's mouth was watering.

Canada's Christmas food tasted like heaven. It was true. But Nigerian Christmas food was the best food on earth! Spicy and savory and mouth-watering . . .

Granny Canada looked at Anna Hibiscus. "Excited about tonight?" she guessed.

Anna Hibiscus nodded. She was very excited. Tonight she was going carol singing in the snow for the very first time!

"But first," said Granny Canada, "the Christmas tree!"

Anna Hibiscus ran to the sink to wash her hands and hang up her apron. Granny Canada brought out the big box of Christmas decorations. Decorations that were already old when Granny Canada was a girl.

Anna Hibiscus was amazed to see tiny candleholders and carved wooden reindeer. There were baubles made of colored glass. And snowflakes baked with cinnamon and painted with glue to make them shiny. Anna Hibiscus and Granny Canada hung them all carefully on the tree.

Last of all was the Christmas angel. Granny Canada held tight to the long ladder, and Anna Hibiscus climbed to the top. Anna Hibiscus carefully tied the angel to the top of the tree with the ribbons behind her big golden wings.

Then Granny Canada and Anna Hibiscus stood back and looked at the beautiful glittering sweet-smelling tree. It was the most beautiful tree Anna had ever seen.

Anna Hibiscus thought again about her family at home in Nigeria.

They too would be busy, in the compound of the big white house. Her big boy cousins would be up ladders, covering every tree and bush and window and balcony in the compound with glittering, twinkling fairy lights. The whole compound would become magical. And loud with Christmas carols played from every radio around.

Anna looked out the window again. Granny Canada's yard was decorated in bright, silent snow.

Anna Hibiscus sighed happily. It was lovely here. And it was wonderful there. Now she was here. But soon she would be back there. Everything was perfect.

"Time to get ready!" Granny Canada said.

Anna Hibiscus ran to put on her most beautiful clothes, ready for the carol singing. She chose the red suit that her African aunties had made especially to keep out the Canada cold. It had a full skirt that twirled when she turned around and a jacket and even a little hat to match.

"You look gorgeous," said Granny Canada. "All red like the winterberries in the snow."

And she lit a candle lantern and took Anna Hibiscus outside, where the candlelight shone out and danced on the snow.

Anna looked down at herself. In Africa she was red like the hibiscus flower, like her name. Here she was red like winterberries in the snow. Anna Hibiscus sighed happily. Again everything was perfect.

Granny Canada took photographs of red-berry Anna all lit up by candlelight and smiling her great-great-grandfather smile. Granny Canada had to wipe her eyes. Maybe because it was so cold.

"Ding dong merrily on high!" rang out voices in the street.

"In heaven the bells are ringing!" Anna Hibiscus joined in loudly.

"Hello, Anna Hibiscus," called Cara and Rosie and Joe.

From street to street and house to house they sang. “Away in a Manger,” “Mary’s Boy Child,” and “Silent Night”—all the carols that Anna Hibiscus knew already. And new ones, like “Jingle Bells” and “Once in Royal David’s City” and “Chestnuts Roasting on an Open Fire,” which she had just learned.

One door was opened by a smiling woman. Anna Hibiscus peeked past into her pretty house. At that same moment, a girl peeked around from behind the woman to see the carol singers!

Anna Hibiscus was so surprised that she stopped singing. The other girl had very curly black hair just like Anna's, and skin the same color as Anna's! She looked just as surprised as Anna Hibiscus did.

Before Anna could say anything, the carol singers started to walk on.

"Glad tidings we bring, to you and your kin," they sang.

Anna Hibiscus kept looking over her shoulder at the smiling woman and the surprised girl until they were gone.

Christmas morning, Anna Hibiscus woke up early. Snow was falling thickly, but Anna was warm in her bed. Cuddled in her arms was the hot-water bottle in its hibiscus flower cover that her mother had knitted for her. And lying over her feet was a warm and heavy snoring shape.

"Qimmiq!" shouted Anna Hibiscus. "It's Christmas!"

Qimmiq stretched up and licked her on the nose!

"Qimmiq!" Anna Hibiscus giggled. "What would Grandfather say!"

It was a good question. Anna Hibiscus did not want to know the answer. What was she going to say to Grandfather about Qimmiq? Anna Hibiscus did not know the answer to that either.

So she jumped out of bed and ran to the kitchen. There above the fire hung her stocking, full and lumpy, and under the tree was a pile of brightly wrapped presents.

Anna shrieked happily. In her stocking were oranges and nuts and chocolate. Anna Hibiscus busied herself with eating them until Granny Canada woke up and made hot chocolate and settled down in front of the fire.

Then Anna Hibiscus opened her presents. There were knitting needles and yarn from Granny Canada. A beautiful red necklace and earrings to match her red suit sent especially from her family in the big white house in Nigeria. And from Cara and Lauren and Tessa and

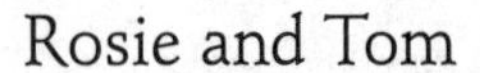

Rosie and Tom

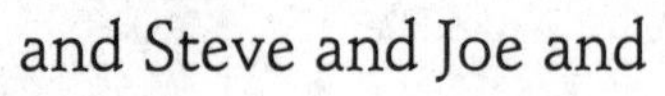

and Steve and Joe and Mark . . . a snow sled of her own!

Anna Hibiscus clapped her hands in delight.

"That will have to live here and wait for your visits," said Granny Canada.

After eating pancakes with maple syrup, Anna Hibiscus and Granny Canada went out to the slope by the lake.

And Granny Canada took videos on Anna's own camera of Anna Hibiscus flying over the snow.

Then they went home to phone the big white house in Nigeria, where everybody would be waking up.

Anna Hibiscus had just finished saying "Merry Christmas! I love you! See you in *two* days!" to everybody when the doorbell rang.

Anna Hibiscus ran to the door. It was the smiling woman and the girl that Anna Hibiscus had seen carol singing! They had come to meet Anna Hibiscus!

"I am Tiger Lily," said the girl shyly.

"And I'm Anna Hibiscus," said Anna. "I'm from Africa."

She waited for Tiger Lily to say that she was from Africa too.

"I'm from Canada," said Tiger Lily.

"Oh," said Anna.

"But in two days I'm going to Africa," Tiger Lily said.

"Me too!" said Anna excitedly.

Tiger Lily was going to visit her father in Africa on the very same day that Anna was going home.

Then they discovered that Anna Hibiscus's father and Tiger Lily's father lived in the very same African city: Lagos, in Nigeria. Which was amazing because Africa is huge and has fifty-five different countries and zillions of cities.

"But I have never been to Africa before," said Tiger Lily, looking very worried.

Anna looked at Tiger Lily's face. She said, "I had not been to Canada before either. I had not even met Granny Canada before I came."

Tiger Lily looked at Anna Hibiscus sitting happily on Granny Canada's lap. She stopped looking so worried.

* * *

And now it was today. Today that Anna Hibiscus was leaving Canada and flying back home to Africa with Tiger Lily and Auntie Jumoke. They were flying on the same plane. Auntie Jumoke had arranged it all.

"Time to go!" called Granny Canada.

Anna Hibiscus threw on her coat, grabbed Double and Trouble's empty pot, and ran outside. At the very last minute, she filled it with snow and packed it into Granny Canada's summer picnic cooler to keep the snow frozen all the way to Africa.

"Bye, Qimmiq," said Anna Hibiscus.

Qimmiq barked. And Anna Hibiscus put her arms around her neck. "You are my best friend," she whispered. "My very best friend!"

Qimmiq barked softly, and Anna Hibiscus burst into tears. All the way to the airport, she cried.

There they met Tiger Lily and her mother. Tiger Lily was crying too.

Auntie Jumoke was waiting for them with one huge overflowing luggage cart. She took one look at the two girls and started to laugh.

"This one," she said, patting Anna Hibiscus's head, "seems to cry before boarding a plane no matter which direction she is headed."

"And this one," said Auntie Jumoke, putting her arm gently around Tiger Lily, "will also be crying when it's time to come back."

Then Auntie Jumoke said to Tiger Lily's mother, "I will personally visit her every day and vouch for her happiness. If she is not happy, I will return her immediately, myself."

So Tiger Lily stopped crying and smiled.

Then Granny Canada bought a big Canada sticker from the airport shop, and Anna Hibiscus stuck it proudly onto the suitcase that Grandfather had given her.

Granny Canada hugged Anna Hibiscus.

"I love you so much, Anna Hibiscus," Granny Canada said. "Come back soon."

"I love you too, Granny Canada," Anna Hibiscus said. "Thank you for telling me all the stories about Great-Great-Grandfather and for making hot chocolate and for Qimmiq—"

Anna Hibiscus burst into tears.

"Time to go!" said Auntie Jumoke.

Auntie Jumoke led them to where only the passengers could go. She loaded them onto the plane. She gave them advice about seat belts and toilets. Then she unpacked her hand luggage. Jollof rice and moi-moi and fried fish and yam balls and hot-hot red spicy stew.

Tiger Lily looked worried.

Anna Hibiscus smiled and opened her bag. She took out the sandwiches and yogurt and chips that Granny Canada had packed for her.

"Have these," she said, giving them to Tiger Lily.

"Are you sure?" asked Tiger Lily.

"Yes," said Anna Hibiscus. Her stomach growled. She could not wait to eat the jollof rice and moi-moi! And she had chocolate cereal in her suitcase. Enough to last her and her cousins for a whole year.

Auntie Jumoke sighed and shook her head as the girls swapped their food.

Tiger Lily smiled.

Cousins or Friends?

Anna Hibiscus was in Canada. Cold, cold Canada. Africa, amazing Africa, was far, far away. But Canada was amazing too.

Anna Hibiscus was sitting in Granny Canada's kitchen-living-dining room. Qimmiq was warm and heavy on her feet. Hot chocolate was steaming under her nose. Granny Canada's knitting needles were *clack-clack-clacking* happily. Anna Hibiscus was writing in her "Adventures of Anna Hibiscus" book. The one her cousins had made for her.

Canada is full of ice and snow. Ice is cold. Snow is cold. Especially when I fell all the way into it. But Canada is COZY too. Cozy means warm and safe and happy. Granny Canada's kitchen is cozy. Good dogs like Qimmiq are cozy.

Anna was writing. And thinking . . . that there was one big *c* word that Canada was not. And that was *cousins*. Canada did not mean cousins.

And Anna Hibiscus—
Anna Hibiscus laughed.